The Most MAGNiFICENT Thing

For all the little perfectionists of the world

Text and illustrations © 2014 Ashley Spires

All rights reserved. No part of this publication may be reproduced, stored in a retrieval system or transmitted, in any form or by any means, without the prior written permission of Kids Can Press Ltd. or, in case of photocopying or other reprographic copying, a license from The Canadian Copyright Licensing Agency (Access Copyright). For an Access Copyright license, visit www.accesscopyright.ca or call toll free to 1-800-893-5777.

Kids Can Press acknowledges the financial support of the Government of Ontario, through the Ontario Media Development Corporation's Ontario Book Initiative; the Ontario Arts Council; the Canada Council for the Arts; and the Government of Canada, through the CBF, for our publishing activity.

Published in Canada by	Published in the U.S. by
Kids Can Press Ltd.	Kids Can Press Ltd.
25 Dockside Drive	2250 Military Road
Toronto, ON M5A 0B5	Tonawanda, NY 14150

www.kidscanpress.com

Kids Can Press is a *corus*™ Entertainment company

The artwork in this book was rendered digitally with lots of practice, two hissy fits and one all-out tantrum.

The text is set in Bookeyed Nelson.

Edited by Yasemin Uçar
Designed by Karen Powers

This book is smyth sewn casebound.
Manufactured in Shenzhen, China, in 3/2016 through Asia Pacific Offset

CM 14 20 19 18 17 16 15 14 13 12

LIBRARY AND ARCHIVES CANADA CATALOGUING IN PUBLICATION

Spires, Ashley, 1978-, author, illustrator

    The most magnificent thing / written and illustrated by Ashley Spires.

    ISBN 978-1-55453-704-4 (bound)

    I. Title.

PS8637.P57M68 2014   jC813'.6   C2013-905840-0

THE MOST MAGNIFICENT THING

Written and illustrated by

Ashley Spires

KIDS CAN PRESS

This is a regular girl and her best friend in the whole wide world.
They do all kinds of things together. They race. They eat. They explore. They relax.

She makes things.

He unmakes things.

One day, the girl has a wonderful idea. She is going to make the most MAGNIFICENT thing!

She knows just how it will look.

She knows just how it will work.

All she has to do is make it, and she makes things all the time. Easy-peasy!

First, she hires an assistant.

Next, they gather their supplies.
They set up somewhere out of the way and get to work.

The girl tinkers and hammers and measures ...

... while her assistant pounces
and growls and chews.

When she is finished, she steps back to admire her work.

She walks around one side. Her assistant examines the other side ...

It doesn't look right. Her assistant picks it up and gives it a shake. It doesn't feel right, either.

They are shocked to discover that the thing isn't magnificent.

Or good. It isn't even kind-of-sort-of okay. It is all WRONG.

The girl tosses it aside and gives it another go.

She smoothes and wrenches and fiddles.

Her assistant circles and tugs and wags.

When she is finished, she stands up and takes a long look at it.
Her assistant gives it a nudge with his paw.

The thing is still wrong. She decides to try again.

The girl saws and glues and adjusts.

She stands and examines and stares.

She twists and tweaks and fastens.

She fixes and straightens and studies.

She tries all different ways to make it better.
She makes it square. She makes it round. She gives it legs. She adds antennae.

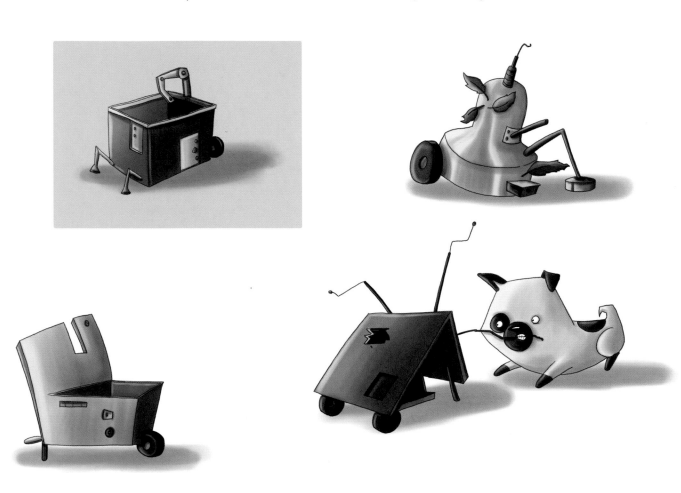

She makes it fuzzy. She makes it long, short, rough, smooth, big, small —
one even smells of stinky cheese! But none of them are MAGNIFICENT.

Her hard work attracts a few admirers, but they don't understand.
They can't see the MAGNIFICENT thing that she has in her mind.

She gets MAD.

The angrier she gets, the faster she works. She SMASHES pieces into shapes.
She JAMS parts together. She PUMMELS the little bits in.

Her hands feel too BIG to work, and her brain is too full of all the not-right things.

If only the thing ... WOULD ... JUST ... WORK!!!

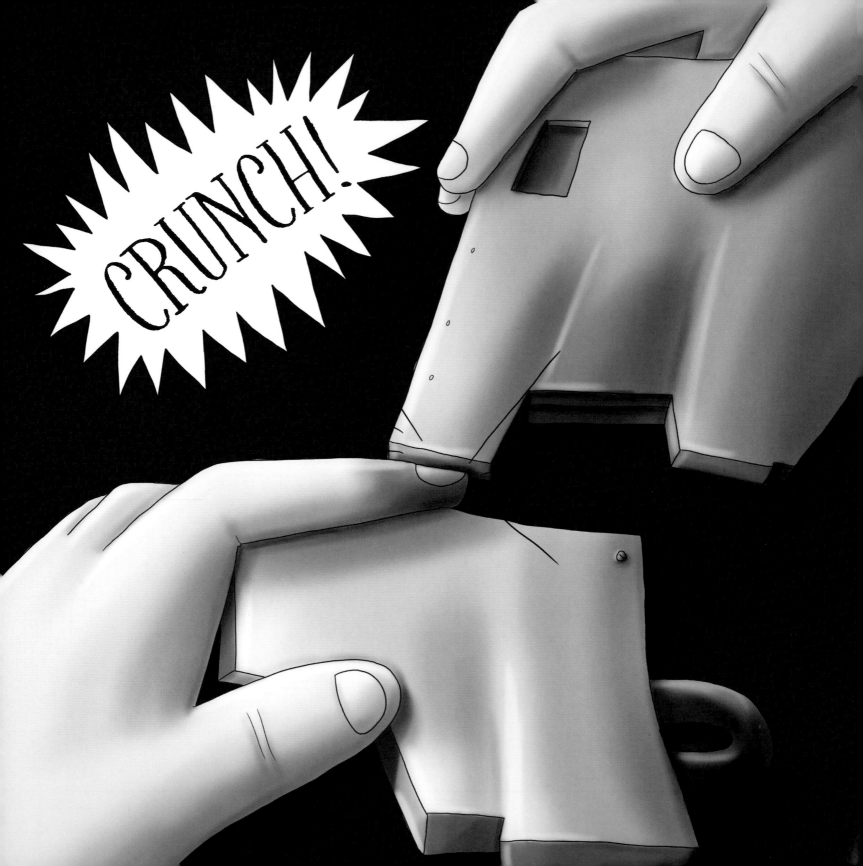

The PAIN starts in her finger.

It rushes up to her BRAIN...

... and she

EXPLODES!

It is not her finest moment.

Her assistant suggests a walk.

It's not much help, at first.

But before long, she starts to feel different.

Bit by bit, the mad gets pushed out of her head.

As they stroll along, she comes across
the first wrong thing she made. The bad
feelings are about to start all over again.
Then she notices something surprising.

There are some parts of the WRONG things that are really quite RIGHT. The bolts on one, the shape of another, the wheel-to-seat ratio of the next. There are all sorts of parts that she likes!

By the time she reaches the end of the trail, she finally knows how to make
the thing MAGNIFICENT. She gets to work. She works carefully and slowly,
tinkering, hammering, twisting, fiddling, gluing, painting ...
Her assistant makes sure there are no distractions.

The afternoon fades into evening. Finally, she finishes.
She alerts her assistant.

The pair take a good, long look.
It leans a little to the left, and it's a bit heavier
than expected. The color could use a bit of work, too.
But it's just what she wanted!

They climb aboard and take it for a spin.
They are not disappointed.
It really is THE MOST MAGNIFICENT THING.